I0648262

William Wordsworth

Intimations of immorality from recollections of early childhood and other poems

William Wordsworth

Intimations of immorality from recollections of early childhood and other poems

ISBN/EAN: 9783337374051

Printed in Europe, USA, Canada, Australia, Japan

Cover: Foto ©Andreas Hilbeck / pixelio.de

More available books at **www.hansebooks.com**

Riverside Literature Series

INTIMATIONS OF IMMORTALITY

FROM RECOLLECTIONS OF EARLY CHILDHOOD
AND OTHER POEMS

BY

WILLIAM WORDSWORTH

WITH BIOGRAPHICAL SKETCH AND NOTES

HOUGHTON, MIFFLIN AND COMPANY
Boston: 4 Park Street; New York: 11 East Seventeenth Street
Chicago: 158 Adams Street
The Riverside Press, Cambridge

Copyright, 1895,
By HOUGHTON, MIFFLIN ، CO.

All rights reserved.

The Riverside Press, Cambridge, Mass., U. S. A.
Electrotyped and Printed by H. O. Houghton and Company.

ALICE FELL;

OR, POVERTY.

Written to gratify Mr. Grahame, of Glasgow, brother of the
author of *The Sabbath*. He was a zealous coadjutor of Mr.
Clarkson, and a man of ardent humanity. The incident had
happened to himself, and he urged me to put it into verse for
humanity's sake. The humbleness, meanness, if you like, of
the subject, together with the homely mode of treating it,
brought upon me a world of ridicule by the small critics, so
that in policy I excluded it from many editions of my poems,
till it was restored at the request of some of my friends, in particular my son-in-law, Edward Quilliuan.

THE post-boy drove with fierce career,
For threatening clouds the moon had drowned,
When, as we hurried on, my ear
Was smitten with a startling sound.

5 As if the wind blew many ways,
I heard the sound, — and more and more;
It seemed to follow with the chaise,
And still I heard it as before.

At length I to the boy called out.
10 He stopped his horses at the word,
But neither cry, nor voice, nor shout,
Nor aught else like it, could be heard.

The boy then smacked his whip, and fast
The horses scampered through the rain ;

15 But, hearing soon upon the blast
The cry, I bade him halt again.

Forthwith alighting on the ground,
" Whence comes," said I, " this piteous moan ? "
And there a little girl I found,
20 Sitting behind the chaise, alone.

" My cloak ! " no other word she spake,
But loud and bitterly she wept,
As if her innocent heart would break ;
And down from off her seat she leapt.

25 " What ails you, child ? "   She sobbed, " Look
here ! "
I saw it in the wheel entangled,
A weather-beaten rag as e'er
From any garden scarecrow dangled.

There, twisted between nave and spoke,
30 It hung, nor could at once be freed ;
But our joint pains unloosed the cloak,
A miserable rag indeed !

" And whither are you going, child,
To-night, along these lonesome ways ? "
35 " To Durham," answered she, half wild.
" Then come with me into the chaise."

Insensible to all relief
Sat the poor girl, and forth did send
Sob after sob, as if her grief
40 Could never, never have an end.

"My child, in Durham do you dwell?"
She checked herself in her distress,
And said, "My name is Alice Fell;
I 'm fatherless and motherless.

45 " And I to Durham, Sir, belong."
Again, as if the thought would choke
Her very heart, her grief grew strong;
And all was for her tattered cloak!

The chaise drove on; our journey's end
50 Was nigh; and, sitting by my side,
As if she had lost her only friend
She wept, nor would be pacified.

Up to the tavern door we post;
Of Alice and her grief I told;
55 And I gave money to the host,
To buy a new cloak for the old.

" And let it be of duffel gray,
As warm a cloak as man can sell!"
Proud creature was she the next day,
60 The little orphan, Alice Fell!

LUCY GRAY;

OR, SOLITUDE.

Oft I had heard of Lucy Gray:
And, when I crossed the wild,
I chanced to see, at break of day,
The solitary child.

5 No mate, no comrade Lucy knew;
She dwelt on a wide moor, —
The sweetest thing that ever grew
Beside a human door!

You yet may spy the fawn at play,
10 The hare upon the green;
But the sweet face of Lucy Gray
Will never more be seen.

"To-night will be a stormy night, —
You to the town must go;
15 And take a lantern, Child, to light
Your mother through the snow."

"That, Father! will I gladly do:
'Tis scarcely afternoon, —
The minster-clock has just struck two,
20 And yonder is the moon!"

At this the father raised his hook,
And snapped a fagot-band;
He plied his work; — and Lucy took
The lantern in her hand.

25 Not blither is the mountain roe:
With many a wanton stroke
Her feet disperse the powdery snow,
That rises up like smoke.

The storm came on before its time:
30 She wandered up and down;
And many a hill did Lucy climb:
But never reached the town.

The wretched parents all that night
Went shouting far and wide;
35 But there was neither sound nor sight
To serve them for a guide.

At daybreak on the hill they stood
That overlooked the moor;
And thence they saw the bridge of wood,
40 A furlong from their door.

They wept, — and, turning homeward, cried,
" In heaven we all shall meet;" —
When in the snow the mother spied
The print of Lucy's feet.

45 Then downwards from the steep hill's edge
They tracked the footmarks small;
And through the broken hawthorn-hedge,
And by the long stone wall;

And then an open field they crossed:
50 The marks were still the same;
They tracked them on, nor ever lost;
And to the bridge they came.

They followed from the snowy bank
Those footmarks, one by one,
55 Into the middle of the plank;
And further there were none!

— Yet some maintain that to this day
She is a living child;
That you may see sweet Lucy Gray
60 Upon the lonesome wild.

O'er rough and smooth she trips along,
And never looks behind ;
And sings a solitary song
That whistles in the wind.

WE ARE SEVEN.

The little girl who is the heroine I met within the area of Go-
derich Castle, in the year 1793. I composed it while walking in
the grove at Alfoxden. My friends will not deem it too trifling
to relate, that while walking to and fro I composed the last
stanza first, having begun with the last line. When it was all
but finished, I came in and recited it to Mr. Coleridge and my
sister, and said, " A prefatory stanza must be added, and I should
sit down to our little tea-meal with greater pleasure if my task
was finished." I mentioned in substance what I wished to be
expressed, and Coleridge immediately threw off the stanza
thus : —

" A little child, dear brother Jem."

I objected to the rhyme, " dear brother Jem," as being ludicrous ;
but we all enjoyed the joke of hitching in our friend James
Tobin's name.

————— A simple Child,
That lightly draws its breath,
And feels its life in every limb,
What should it know of death ?

5 I met a little cottage girl :
She was eight years old, she said ;
Her hair was thick with many a curl
That clustered round her head.

She had a rustic, woodland air,
10 And she was wildly clad :
Her eyes were fair, and very fair ; —
Her beauty made me glad.

"Sisters and brothers, little Maid,
How many may you be?"
15 "How many? Seven in all," she said,
And wondering looked at me.

"And where are they? I pray you tell."
She answered, "Seven are we;
And two of us at Conway dwell,
20 And two are gone to sea.

"Two of us in the churchyard lie,
My sister and my brother;
And, in the churchyard cottage, I
Dwell near them with my mother."

25 "You say that two at Conway dwell,
And two are gone to sea,
Yet ye are seven! I pray you tell,
Sweet Maid, how this may be."

Then did the little Maid reply,
30 "Seven boys and girls are we;
Two of us in the churchyard lie,
Beneath the churchyard tree."

"You run about, my little Maid,
Your limbs they are alive;
35 If two are in the churchyard laid
Then ye are only five."

"Their graves are green, they may be seen,"
The little Maid replied,
"Twelve steps or more from my mother's door,
40 And they are side by side.

" My stockings there I often knit,
My kerchief there I hem ;
And there upon the ground I sit
And sing a song to them.

45 " And often after sunset, Sir,
When it is light and fair,
I take my little porringer,
And eat my supper there.

" The first that died was sister Jane ;
50 In bed she moaning lay,
Till God released her of her pain ;
And then she went away.

" So in the churchyard she was laid ;
And, when the grass was dry,
55 Together round her grave we played,
My brother John and I.

" And when the ground was white with snow
And I could run and slide,
My brother John was forced to go,
60 And he lies by her side."

" How many are you, then," said I,
" If they two are in heaven ? "
Quick was the little Maid's reply,
" O Master ! we are seven."

65 " But they are dead ; those two are dead !
Their spirits are in heaven ! "
'T was throwing words away ; for still
The little Maid would have her will,
And said, " Nay, we are seven ! "

THE PET LAMB.

A PASTORAL.

THE dew was falling fast, the stars began to blink;
I heard a voice; it said, " Drink, pretty creature,
    drink ! "
And, looking o'er the hedge, before me I espied
A snow-white mountain-lamb with a maiden at its
    side.

5 Nor sheep nor kine were near; the lamb was all
    alone,
And by a slender cord was tethered to a stone;
With one knee on the grass did the little maiden
    kneel,
While to that mountain-lamb she gave its evening
    meal.

The lamb, while from her hand he thus his supper
    took,
10 Seemed to feast with head and ears; and his tail
    with pleasure shook.
" Drink, pretty creature, drink ! " she said, in such
    a tone
That I almost received her heart into my own.

'T was little Barbara Lewthwaite, a child of beauty
    rare !
I watched them with delight, they were a lovely
    pair.
15 Now with her empty can the maiden turned away,
But ere ten yards were gone, her footsteps did she
    stay.

Right towards the lamb she looked ; and from a
    shady place
I unobserved could see the workings of her face :
If nature to her tongue could measured numbers
    bring,
20 Thus, thought I, to her lamb that little maid might
    sing : —

" What ails thee, young one ? what ? Why pull so
    at thy cord ?
Is it not well with thee ? well both for bed and
    board ?
Thy plot of grass is soft, and green as grass can
    be ;
Rest, little young one, rest ; what is 't that aileth
    thee ?

25 " What is it thou wouldst seek ? What is wanting
    to thy heart ?
Thy limbs, are they not strong ? And beautiful
    thou art :
This grass is tender grass ; these flowers they have
    no peers ;
And that green cord all day is rustling in thy ears !

" If the sun be shining hot, do but stretch thy wool-
    len chain,
30 This beech is standing by, its covert thou canst
    gain ;
For rain and mountain-storms ! the like thou need'st
    not fear,
The rain and storm are things that scarcely can
    come here.

" Rest, little young one, rest; thou hast forgot the
day
When my father found thee first in places far
away;
35 Many flocks were on the hills, but thou wert owned
by none,
And thy mother from thy side for evermore was
gone.

" He took thee in his arms, and in pity brought
thee home :
A blessed day for thee ! then whither wouldst thou
roam ?
A faithful nurse thou hast; the dam that did thee
yean
40 Upon the mountain - tops no kinder could have
been.

" Thou know'st that twice a day I have brought
thee in this can
Fresh water from the brook, as clear as ever ran;
And twice in the day, when the ground is wet with
dew,
I bring thee draughts of milk, — warm milk it is
and new.

45 " Thy limbs will shortly be twice as stout as they
are now,
Then I 'll yoke thee to my cart like a pony in the
plough;
My playmate thou shalt be ; and when the wind is
cold,
Our hearth shall be thy bed, our house shall be thy
fold.

" It will not, will not rest ! — Poor creature, can it be
50 That 't is thy mother's heart which is working so in
  thee ?
Things that I know not of belike to thee are dear,
And dreams of things which thou canst neither see
  nor hear.

" Alas, the mountain-tops that look so green and
  fair !
I 've heard of fearful winds and darkness that come
  there ;
55 The little brooks that seem all pastime and all play
When they are angry roar like lions for their prey.

" Here thou need'st not dread the raven in the sky ;
Night and day thou art safe, — our cottage is hard
  by.
Why bleat so after me ?   Why pull so at thy chain ?
60 Sleep, — and at break of day I will come to thee
  again ! "

— As homeward through the lane I went with lazy
  feet,
This song to myself did I oftentimes repeat ;
And it seemed, as I retraced the ballad line by line,
That but half of it was hers, and one half of it was
  mine.

65 Again, and once again, did I repeat the song ;
" Nay," said I, " more than half to the damsel must
  belong,
For she looked with such a look, and she spake
  with such a tone,
That I almost received her heart into my own."

THE IDLE SHEPHERD–BOYS;

OR, DUNGEON-GHYLL FORCE.[1]

A PASTORAL.

THE valley rings with mirth and joy;
Among the hills the echoes play
A never, never ending song,
To welcome in the May.
5 The magpie chatters with delight;
The mountain raven's youngling brood
Have left the mother and the nest;
And they go rambling east and west
In search of their own food;
10 Or through the glittering vapors dart
In very wantonness of heart.

Beneath a rock, upon the grass,
Two boys are sitting in the sun;
Their work, if any work they have,
15 Is out of mind, — or done.
On pipes of sycamore they play
The fragments of a Christmas hymn;
Or with that plant which in our dale
We call stag-horn, or fox's tail,
20 Their rusty hats they trim:
And thus, as happy as the day,
Those shepherds wear the time away.

Along the river's stony marge
The sand-lark chants a joyous song;

---

[1] **Ghyll**, in the dialect of Cumberland and Westmoreland, is a short, and for the most part a steep, narrow valley, with a stream running through it. *Force* is the word universally employed in these dialects for waterfall. — W. W.

25 The thrush is busy in the wood,
And carols loud and strong.
A thousand lambs are on the rocks,
All newly born! both earth and sky
Keep jubilee, and more than all,
30 Those boys with their green coronal;
They never hear the cry,
That plaintive cry! which up the hill
Comes from the depth of Dungeon-Ghyll.

Said Walter, leaping from the ground,
35 " Down to the stump of yon old yew
We 'll for our whistles run a race."
———Away the shepherds flew;
They leapt, — they ran, — and when they came
Right opposite to Dungeon-Ghyll,
40 Seeing that he should lose the prize,
" Stop!" to his comrade Walter cries.
James stopped with no good will:
Said Walter then, exulting, " Here
You 'll find a task for half a year.

45 " Cross, if you dare, where I shall cross, —
Come on, and tread where I shall tread."
The other took him at his word,
And followed as he led.
It was a spot which you may see
50 If ever you to Langdale go;
Into the chasm a mighty block
Hath fallen, and made a bridge of rock;
The gulf is deep below;
And, in a basin black and small,
55 Receives a lofty waterfall.

With staff in hand across the cleft
The challenger pursued his march;
And now, all eyes and feet, hath gained
The middle of the arch.
60 When list! he hears a piteous moan.
Again! — his heart within him dies;
His pulse is stopped, his breath is lost,
He totters, pallid as a ghost,
And, looking down, espies
65 A lamb, that in the pool is pent
Within that black and frightful rent.

The lamb had slipped into the stream,
And safe without a bruise or wound
The cataract had borne him down
70 Into the gulf profound.
His dam had seen him when he fell,
She saw him down the torrent borne;
And, while with all a mother's love
She from the lofty rocks above
75 Sent forth a cry forlorn,
The lamb, still swimming round and round,
Made answer in that plaintive sound.

When he had learnt what thing it was
That sent this rueful cry, I ween
80 The boy recovered heart, and told
The sight which he had seen.
Both gladly now deferred their task;
Nor was there wanting other aid:
A poet, one who loves the brooks
85 Far better than the sages' books,
By chance had hither strayed;
And there the helpless lamb he found
By those hugh rocks encompassed round.

He drew it from the troubled pool,
90 And brought it forth into the light :
The shepherds met him with his charge,
An unexpected sight !
Into their arms the lamb they took,
Whose life and limbs the flood had spared ;
95 Then up the steep ascent they hied,
And placed him at his mother's side ;
And gently did the bard
Those idle shepherd-boys upbraid,
And bade them better mind their trade.

RURAL ARCHITECTURE.

THERE 's George Fisher, Charles Fleming, and
Reginald Shore,
Three rosy-cheeked schoolboys, the highest not
more
Than the height of a counsellor's bag.
To the top of GREAT HOW[1] did it please them to
climb :
5 And there they built up, without mortar or lime,
A Man on the peak of the crag.

They built him of stones gathered up as they lay ;
They built him and christened him all in one day,
An urchin both vigorous and hale ;
10 And so without scruple they called him Ralph
Jones.

4. **Great How** is a single and conspicuous hill, which rises
towards the foot of Thirlmere, on the western side of the beautiful dale of Legberthwaite, along the higu road between Keswick
and Ambleside. — W. W.

Now Ralph is renowned for the length of his bones ;
The Magog of Legberthwaite dale.

Just half a week after, the wind sallied forth,
And, in anger or merriment, out of the north,
15 Coming on with a terrible pother,
From the peak of the crag blew the giant away.
And what did these schoolboys ? — The very next
    day
They went and they built up another.

— Some little I 've seen of blind boisterous works
20 By Christian disturbers more savage than Turks,
Spirits busy to do and undo :
At rememberance whereof my blood sometimes will
    flag ;
Then, light-hearted boys, to the top of the crag ;
And I 'll build up a giant with you.

THE REVERIE OF POOR SUSAN.

This arose out of my observation of the affecting music of
these birds, hanging in this way in the London streets, during
the freshness and stillness of the spring morning.

At the corner of Wood Street, when daylight
    appears,
Hangs a thrush that sings loud, it has sung for
    three years :
Poor Susan has passed by the spot, and has heard
In the silence of morning the song of the bird.

5 'T is a note of enchantment ; what ails her ? She sees
A mountain ascending, a vision of trees ;

Bright volumes of vapor through Lothbury glide,
And a river flows on through the vale of Cheapside.

Green pastures she views in the midst of the dale,
10 Down which she so often has tripped with her pail,
And a single small cottage, a nest like a dove's,
The one only dwelling on earth that she loves.

She looks, and her heart is in heaven : but they fade,
The mist and the river, the hill and the shade :
15 The stream will not flow, and the hill will not rise,
And the colors have all passed away from her eyes!

POWER OF MUSIC.

An Orpheus! an Orpheus! yes, Faith may grow
    bold,
And take to herself all the wonders of old; —
Near the stately Pantheon you'll meet with the
    same
In the street that from Oxford hath borrowed its
    name.

5 His station is there; and he works on the crowd,
He sways them with harmony merry and loud ;
He fills with his power all their hearts to the
    brim, —
Was aught ever heard like his fiddle and him?

7. **Lothbury** and **Cheapside** are streets in the heart of the
city of London.

1. **Orpheus** was the hero in Greek mythology whose music
was so powerful that even the stones fell into place in building
when he played on his lyre.

What an eager assembly! what an empire is this!
10 The weary have life, and the hungry have bliss;
The mourner is cheered, and the anxious have rest;
And the guilt-burdened soul is no longer opprest.

As the moon brightens round her the clouds of the
    night,
So he, where he stands, is a centre of light;
15 It gleams on the face, there, of dusky-browed Jack,
And the pale-visaged baker's, with basket on back.

That errand-bound 'prentice was passing in haste, —
What matter! he 's caught, — and his time runs to
    waste;
The newsman is stopped, though he stops on the
    fret;
20 And the half-breathless lamp-lighter, — he 's in the
    net!

The porter sits down on the weight which he bore;
The lass with her barrow wheels hither her store; —
If a thief could be here, he might pilfer at ease;
She sees the musician, 't is all that she sees!

25 He stands, backed by the wall; — he abates not his
    din; —
His hat gives him vigor, with boons dropping in,
From the old and the young, from the poorest; and
    there!
The one-pennied boy has his penny to spare.

Oh, blest are the hearers, and proud be the hand
30 Of the pleasure it spreads through so thankful a
    band!

I am glad for him, blind as he is! — all the while
If they speak 't is to praise, and they praise with a
smile.

That tall man, a giant in bulk and in height,
Not an inch of his body is free from delight ;
35 Can he keep himself still, if he would ?   Oh, not
he !
The music stirs in him like wind through a tree.

Mark that cripple who leans on his crutch ; like a
tower
That long has leaned forward, leans hour after
hour !
That mother, whose spirit in fetters is bound,
40.While she dandles the babe in her arms to the
sound.

Now, coaches and chariots ! roar on like a stream ;
Here are twenty souls happy as souls in a dream :
They are deaf to your murmurs, — they care not
for you,
Nor what ye are flying, nor what ye pursue !

TO A BUTTERFLY.

FIRST POEM.

My sister and I were parted immediately after the death of
our mother, who died in March, 1778, both being very young.

STAY near me ; do not take thy flight !
A little longer stay in sight !
Much converse do I find in thee,
Historian of my infancy !

5 Float near me ; do not yet depart!
Dead times revive in thee :
Thou bring'st, gay creature as thou art!
A solemn image to my heart,
My father's family!

10 Oh! pleasant, pleasant were the days,
The time, when, in our childish plays,
My sister Emmeline and I
Together chased the butterfly!
A very hunter did I rush
15 Upon the prey : — with leaps and springs
I followed on from brake to bush ;
But she, God love her! feared to brush
The dust from off its wings.

SECOND POEM.

I 've watched you now a full half hour
Self-poised upon that yellow flower ;
And, little Butterfly! indeed
I know not if you sleep or feed.
5 How motionless! — not frozen seas
More motionless! — and then
What joy awaits you, when the breeze
Hath found you out among the trees,
And calls you forth again!

10 This plot of orchard-ground is ours ;
My trees they are, my sister's flowers :
Here rest your wings when they are weary,
Here lodge as in a sanctuary!
Come often to us, fear no wrong ;
15 Sit near us on the bough!

We 'll talk of sunshine and of song,
And summer days, when we were young;
Sweet childish days, that were as long
As twenty days are now.

THE SPARROW'S NEST.

Behold, within the leafy shade,
Those bright blue eggs together laid!
On me the chance-discovered sight
Gleamed like a vision of delight.
5 I started, — seeming to espy
The home and sheltered bed,
The sparrow's dwelling, which, hard by
My father's house, in wet or dry,
My sister Emmeline and I
10   Together visited.

She looked at it and seemed to fear it;
Dreading, tho' wishing, to be near it:
Such heart was in her, being then
A little prattler among men.
15 The blessing of my later years
Was with me when a boy:
She gave me eyes, she gave me ears;
And humble cares, and delicate fears;
A heart, the fountain of sweet tears;
20   And love, and thought, and joy.

TO A SKYLARK.

FIRST POEM.

Up with me! up with me into the clouds!
  For thy song, Lark, is strong;
Up with me! up with me into the clouds!
  Singing, singing,
5 With clouds and sky about thee ringing,
  Lift me, guide me till I find
That spot which seems so to thy mind!

I have walked through wildernesses dreary,
And to-day my heart is weary;
10 Had I now the wings of a Faery,
  Up to thee would I fly.
There is madness about thee, and joy **divine**
  In that song of thine;
Lift me, guide me high and high
15 To thy banqueting-place in the sky.

    Joyous as morning,
Thou art laughing and scorning;
Thou hast a nest for thy love and thy **rest**,
And, though little troubled with sloth,
20 Drunken Lark! thou wouldst be loth
  To be such a traveller as I.
Happy, happy liver,
With a soul as strong as a mountain river
Pouring out praise to the Almighty Giver,
25   Joy and jollity be with us both!

20. So we sometimes say that one is intoxicated with joy.

Alas! my journey, rugged and uneven,
Through prickly moors or dusty ways must wind ;
But hearing thee, or others of thy kind,
As full of gladness and as free of heaven,
30 I, with my fate contented, will plod on,
And hope for higher raptures, when life's day is
done.

SECOND POEM.

ETHEREAL minstrel! pilgrim of the sky!
Dost thou despise the earth where cares abound?
Or, while the wings aspire, are heart and eye
Both with thy nest upon the dewy ground?
5 Thy nest, which thou canst drop into at will,
Those quivering wings composed, that music still.

Leave to the nightingale her shady wood ;
A privacy of glorious light is thine ;
Whence thou dost pour upon the world a flood
10 Of harmony, with instinct more divine ;
Type of the wise who soar, but never roam ;
True to the kindred points of Heaven and Home.

TO A NIGHTINGALE.

O NIGHTINGALE! thou surely art
A creature of a " fiery heart : " —
These notes of thine, — they pierce and pierce :
Tumultuous harmony and fierce !
5 Thou sing'st as if the God of wine
Had helped thee to a Valentine ;
A song in mockery and despite
Of shades, and dews, and silent night ;

And steady bliss, and all the loves
10 Now sleeping in these peaceful groves.
I heard a stock-dove sing or say
His homely tale, this very day ;
His voice was buried among trees,
Yet to be come at by the breeze :
15 He did not cease ; but cooed — and cooed ;
And somewhat pensively he wooed :
He sang of love, with quiet blending,
Slow to begin, and never ending ;
Of serious faith, and inward glee ;
20 That was the song, — the song for me !

TO THE CUCKOO.

O BLITHE New-comer ! I have heard,
I hear thee and rejoice.
O Cuckoo ! shall I call thee Bird,
Or but a wandering Voice ?

5 While I am lying on the grass
Thy twofold shout I hear,
From hill to hill it seems to pass,
At once far off, and near.

Though babbling only to the vale,
10 Of sunshine and of flowers,
Thou bringest unto me a tale
Of visionary hours.

Thrice welcome, darling of the Spring !
Even yet thou art to me
15 No bird, but an invisible thing,
A voice, a mystery ;

The same whom in my schoolboy days
I listened to ; that cry
Which made me look a thousand ways,
20 In bush, and tree, and sky.

To seek thee did I often rove
Through woods and on the green ;
And thou wert still a hope, a love ;
Still longed for, never seen.

25 And I can listen to thee yet ;
Can lie upon the plain
And listen, till I do beget
That golden time again.

O blessed Bird ! the earth we pace
30 Again appears to be
An unsubstantial, faery place ;
That is fit home for thee !

SHE WAS A PHANTOM OF DELIGHT.

SHE was a phantom of delight
When first she gleamed upon my sight ;
A lovely apparition, sent
To be a moment's ornament ;
5 Her eyes as stars of twilight fair ;
Like twilight's, too, her dusky hair ;
But all things else about her drawn
From May-time and the cheerful dawn ;
A dancing shape, an image gay,
10 To haunt, to startle, and waylay.

I saw her upon nearer view,
A spirit, yet a woman too!
Her household motions light and free,
And steps of virgin liberty;
15 A countenance in which did meet
Sweet records, promises as sweet;
A creature not too bright or good
For human nature's daily food;
For transient sorrows, simple wiles,
20 Praise, blame, love, kisses, tears, and smiles.

And now I see with eye serene
The very pulse of the machine;
A being breathing thoughtful breath,
A traveller between life and death;
25 The reason firm, the temperate will,
Endurance, foresight, strength, and skill;
A perfect woman, nobly planned,
To warn, to comfort, and command;
And yet a spirit still, and bright
30 With something of angelic light.

THREE YEARS SHE GREW.

THREE years she grew in sun and shower:
Then Nature said, " A lovelier flower
On earth was never sown;
This child I to myself will take;
5 She shall be mine, and I will make
A lady of my own.

"Myself will to my darling be
Both law and impulse : and with me

The girl, in rock and plain,
10 In earth and heaven, in glade and bower,
Shall feel an overseeing power
To kindle or restrain.

" She shall be sportive as the fawn
That wild with glee across the lawn
15 Or up the mountain springs ;
And hers shall be the breathing balm,
And hers the silence and the calm
Of mute, insensate things.

" The floating clouds their state shall lend
20 To her ; for her the willow bend ;
Nor shall she fail to see,
Even in the motions of the storm,
Grace that shall mould the maiden's form
By silent sympathy.

25 " The stars of midnight shall be dear
To her ; and she shall lean her ear
In many a secret place
Where rivulets dance their wayward round,
And beauty born of murmuring sound
30 Shall pass into her face.

" And vital feelings of delight
Shall rear her form to stately height,
Her virgin bosom swell ;
Such thoughts to Lucy I will give
35 While she and I together live
Here in this happy dell."

Thus Nature spake. — The work was done. —
How soon my Lucy's race was run!
She died, and left to me
40 This heath, this calm and quiet scene;
The memory of what has been,
And never more will be.

SHE DWELT AMONG THE UNTRODDEN WAYS.

SHE dwelt among the untrodden ways
  Beside the springs of Dove,
A maid whom there were none to praise,
  And very few to love:

5 A violet by a mossy stone
  Half hidden from the eye!
Fair as a star, when only one
  Is shining in the sky.

She lived unknown, and few could know
10   When Lucy ceased to be;
But she is in her grave, and oh!
  The difference to me!

A SLUMBER DID MY SPIRIT SEAL.

A SLUMBER did my spirit seal;
  I had no human fears:
She seemed a thing that could not feel
  The touch of earthly years.

5 No motion has she now, no force ;
  She neither hears nor sees ;
Rolled round in earth's diurnal course,
  With rocks, and stones, and trees.

I TRAVELLED AMONG UNKNOWN MEN.

I TRAVELLED among unknown men,
  In lands beyond the sea ;
Nor, England ! did I know till then
  What love I bore to thee.

5 'T is past, that melancholy dream !
  Nor will I quit thy shore
A second time ; for still I seem
  To love thee more and more.

Among thy mountains did I feel
10   The joy of my desire ;
And she I cherished turned her wheel
  Beside an English fire.

Thy morning showed, thy nights concealed,
  The bowers where Lucy played ;
15 And thine too is the last green field
  That Lucy's eyes surveyed.

THE DAFFODILS.

I WANDERED lonely as a cloud
That floats on high o'er vales and hills,
When all at once I saw a crowd,
A host, of golden daffodils;
5 Beside the lake, beneath the trees,
Fluttering and dancing in the breeze.

Continuous as the stars that shine
And twinkle on the milky way,
They stretched in never-ending line
10 Along the margin of a bay:
Ten thousand saw I at a glance,
Tossing their heads in sprightly dance.

The waves beside them danced; but they
Outdid the sparkling waves in glee:
15 A poet could not but be gay,
In such a jocund company:
I gazed, — and gazed, — but little thought
What wealth the show to me had brought:

For oft, when on my couch I lie
20 In vacant or in pensive mood,
They flash upon that inward eye
Which is the bliss of solitude;
And then my heart with pleasure fills,
And dances with the daffodils.

TO THE DAISY.

"Her[1] divine skill taught me this,
That from everything I saw
I could some instruction draw,
And raise pleasure to the height
Through the meanest object's sight.
By the murmur of a spring,
Or the least bough's rustelling;
By a Daisy whose leaves spread
Shut when Titan goes to bed;
Or a shady bush or tree;
She could more infuse in me,
Than all Nature's beauties can
In some other wiser man."

G. WITHER.

In youth from rock to rock I went,
From hill to hill, in discontent
Of pleasure high and turbulent,
    Most pleased when most uneasy;
5 But now my own delights I make, —
My thirst at every rill can slake,
And gladly Nature's love partake,
    Of thee, sweet Daisy!

Thee Winter in the garland wears
10 That thinly decks his few gray hairs;
Spring parts the clouds with softest airs,
    That she may sun thee;
Whole Summer-fields are thine by right;
And Autumn, melancholy wight!
15 Doth in thy crimson head delight
    When rains are on thee.

In shoals and bands, a morrice train,
Thou greet'st the traveller in the lane;
Pleased at his greeting thee again;
20   Yet nothing daunted,

[1] His Muse.

Nor grieved, if thou be set at naught:
And oft alone in nooks remote
We meet thee, like a pleasant thought,
    When such are wanted.

25 Be violets in their sacred mews
The flowers the wanton zephyrs choose;
Proud be the rose, with rains and dews
    Her head impearling;
Thou liv'st with less ambitious aim,
30 Yet hast not gone without thy fame;
Thou art indeed by many a claim
    The poet's darling.

If to a rock from rains he fly,
Or, some bright day of April sky,
35 Imprisoned by hot sunshine lie
    Near the green holly,
And wearily at length should fare;
He needs but look about, and there
Thou art!—a friend at hand, to scare
40   His melancholy.

A hundred times, by rock or bower,
Ere thus I have lain couched an hour,
Have I derived from thy sweet power
    Some apprehension;
45 Some steady love; some brief delight;
Some memory that had taken flight;
Some chime of fancy wrong or right;
    Or stray invention.

If stately passions in me burn,
50 And one chance look to thee should turn,

I drink out of an humbler urn
    A lowlier pleasure;
The homely sympathy that heeds
The common life, our nature breeds;
55 A wisdom fitted to the needs
    Of hearts at leisure.

Fresh-smitten by the morning ray,
When thou art up, alert and gay,
Then, cheerful Flower! my spirits play
60   With kindred gladness:
And when, at dusk, by dews opprest
Thou sink'st, the image of thy rest
Hath often eased my pensive breast
    Of careful sadness.

65 And all day long I number yet,
All seasons through, another debt,
Which I, wherever thou art met,
    To thee am owing;
An instinct call it, a blind sense;
70 A happy, genial influence,
Coming one knows not how, nor whence,
    Nor whither going.

Child of the Year! that round dost run
Thy pleasant course, — when day's begun
75 As ready to salute the sun
    As lark or leveret,
Thy long-lost praise thou shalt regain;
Nor be less dear to future men
Than in old time; — thou not in vain
80   Art Nature's favorite.

80. See, in Chaucer and the elder poets, the honors formerly
paid to this flower. — W. W.

TO THE SAME FLOWER.

WITH little here to do or see
Of things that in the great world be,
Daisy! again I talk to thee,
    For thou art worthy,
5 Thou unassuming Commonplace
Of Nature, with that homely face,
And yet with something of a grace,
    Which Love makes for thee!

Oft on the dappled turf at ease
10 I sit, and play with similes,
Loose types of things through all degrees,
    Thoughts of thy raising:
And many a fond and idle name
I give to thee, for praise or blame,
15 As is the humor of the game,
    While I am gazing.

A nun demure, of lowly port:
Or sprightly maiden, of Love's court,
In thy simplicity the sport
20   Of all temptations;
A queen in crown of rubies drest;
A starveling in a scanty vest;
Are all, as seems to suit thee best,
    Thy appellations.

25 A little cyclops, with one eye
Staring to threaten and defy,
That thought comes next, — and instantly
    The freak is over,

The shape will vanish, — and behold
30 A silver shield with boss of gold,
That spreads itself, some faery bold
    In fight to cover !

I see thee glittering from afar, —
And then thou art a pretty star ;
35 Not quite so fair as many are
    In heaven above thee !
Yet like a star, with glittering crest,
Self-poised in air thou seem'st to rest ; —
May peace come never to his nest,
40   Who shall reprove thee !

Bright *Flower !* for by that name at last,
When all my reveries are past,
I call thee, and to that cleave fast,
    Sweet, silent creature !
45 That breath'st with me in sun and air,
Do thou, as thou art wont, repair
My heart with gladness, and a share
    Of thy meek nature !

TO THE SMALL CELANDINE.

It is remarkable that this flower, coming out so early in the
spring as it does, and so bright and beautiful, and in such pro-
fusion, should not have been noticed earlier in English verse.
What adds much to the interest that attends it is its habit of
shutting itself up and opening out according to the degree of
light and temperature of the air.

PANSIES, lilies, kingcups, daisies,
Let them live upon their praises ;
Long as there 's a sun that sets,
Primroses will have their glory ;

5 Long as there are violets,
They will have a place in story :
There 's a flower that shall be mine.
'T is the little Celandine.

Eyes of some men travel far
10 For the finding of a star ;
Up and down the heavens they go,
Men that keep a mighty rout !
I 'm as great as they, I trow,
Since the day I found thee out,
15 Little flower ! — I 'll make a stir,
Like a sage astronomer.

Modest, yet withal an elf
Bold, and lavish of thyself ;
Since we needs must first have met,
20 I have seen thee, high and low,
Thirty years or more, and yet
'T was a face I did not know :
Thou hast now, go where I may,
Fifty greetings in a day.

25 Ere a leaf is on a bush,
In the time before the thrush
Has a thought about her nest,
Thou wilt come with half a call,
Spreading out thy glossy breast
30 Like a careless prodigal ;
Telling tales about the sun,
When we 've little warmth, or none.

Poets, vain men in their mood !
Travel with the multitude :

8. Common pilewort.

35 Never heed them; I aver
That they all are wanton wooers;
But the thrifty cottager,
Who stirs little out of doors,
Joys to spy thee near at home;
40 Spring is coming, thou art come!

Comfort have thou of thy merit,
Kindly, unassuming spirit!
Careless of thy neighborhood,
Thou dost show thy pleasant face
45 On the moor, and in the wood,
In the lane; — there 's not a place,
Howsoever mean it be,
But 't is good enough for thee.

Ill befall the yellow flowers,
50 Children of the flaring hours!
Buttercups, that will be seen,
Whether we will see or no;
Others, too, of lofty mien;
They have done as worldlings do,
55 Taken praise that should be thine,
Little, humble Celandine.

Prophet of delight and mirth,
Ill-requited upon earth;
Herald of a mighty band,
60 Of a joyous train ensuing,
Serving at my heart's command,
Tasks that are no tasks renewing,
I will sing, as doth behoove,
Hymns in praise of what I love!

TO MY SISTER.

I<small>T</small> is the first mild day of March:
Each minute sweeter than before.
The redbreast sings from the tall larch
That stands beside our door.

5 There is a blessing in the air,
  Which seems a sense of joy to yield
To the bare trees, and mountains bare,
  And grass in the green field.

My sister! ('t is a wish of mine,)
10 Now that our morning meal is done,
Make haste, your morning task resign;
  Come forth and feel the sun.

Edward will come with you; — and, pray,
Put on with speed your woodland dress;
15 And bring no book: for this one day
  We 'll give to idleness.

No joyless forms shall regulate
  Our living calendar:
We from to-day, my friend, will date
20 The opening of the year.

Love, now a universal birth,
From heart to heart is stealing,
From earth to man, from man to earth,
  — It is the hour of feeling.

25 One moment now may give us more
  Than years of toiling reason:

Our minds shall drink at every pore
The spirit of the season.

Some silent laws our hearts will make,
30 Which they shall long obey :
We for the year to come may 'take
Our temper from to-day.

And from the blessed power that rolls
About, below, above,
35 We 'll frame the measure of our souls :
They shall be tuned to love.

Then come, my sister ! come, I pray ;
With speed put on your woodland dress,
And bring no book : for this one day
40 We 'll give to idleness.

SONNET.

Most sweet it is with unuplifted eyes
To pace the ground, if path be there or none,
While a fair region round the traveller lies
Which he forbears again to look upon ;
5 Pleased rather with some soft ideal scene,
The work of fancy, or some happy tone
Of meditation, slipping in between
The beauty coming and the beauty gone.
If thought and love desert us, from that day
10 Let us break off all commerce with the Muse :
With thought and love companions of our way,
Whate'er the senses take or may refuse,
The mind's internal heaven shall shed her dews
Of inspiration on the humblest lay.

EXPOSTULATION AND REPLY.

" Why, William, on that old gray stone,
Thus for the length of half a day,
Why, William, sit you thus alone,
And dream your time away ?

5 " Where are your books ? — that light bequeathed
To beings else forlorn and blind !
Up ! up ! and drink the spirit breathed
From dead men to their kind.

" You look round on your Mother Earth,
10 As if she for no purpose bore you ;
As if you were her first-born birth,
And none had lived before you ! "

One morning thus, by Esthwaite lake,
When life was sweet, I knew not why,
15 To me my good friend Matthew spake,
And thus I made reply : —

" The eye, — it cannot choose but see ;
We cannot bid the year be still ;
Our bodies feel, where'er they be,
20 Against or with our will.

" Nor less I deem that there are powers
Which of themselves our minds impress ;
That we can feed this mind of ours
In a wise passiveness.

25 " Think you, 'mid all this mighty sum
Of things forever speaking,

That nothing of itself will come,
But we must still be seeking?

"Then ask not wherefore, here, alone,
30 Conversing as I may,
I sit upon this old gray stone,
And dream my time away."

THE TABLES TURNED.

AN EVENING SCENE ON THE SAME SUBJECT.

UP! up! my friend, and quit your books,
Or surely you'll grow double:
Up! up! my friend, and clear your looks;
Why all this toil and trouble?

5 The sun, above the mountain's head,
A freshening lustre mellow
Through all the long, green fields has spread,
His first sweet evening yellow.

Books! 't is a dull and endless strife:
10 Come, hear the woodland linnet,
How sweet his music! on my life,
There's more of wisdom in it.

And hark! how blithe the throstle sings!
He, too, is no mean preacher:
15 Come forth into the light of things,
Let Nature be your teacher.

She has a world of ready wealth,
Our minds and hearts to bless, —

Spontaneous wisdom breathed by health,
20 Truth breathed by cheerfulness.

One impulse from a vernal wood
May teach you more of man,
Of moral evil and of good,
Than all the sages can.

25 Sweet is the lore which Nature brings;
Our meddling intellect
Misshapes the beauteous forms of things, —
We murder to dissect.

Enough of Science and of Art;
30 Close up those barren leaves;
Come forth, and bring with you a heart
That watches and receives.

SONNET.

THE world is too much with us; late and soon,
Getting and spending, we lay waste our powers:
Little we see in Nature that is ours;
We have given our hearts away, a sordid boon!
5 This sea that bares her bosom to the moon;
The winds that will be howling at all hours,
And are up-gathered now like sleeping flowers;
For this, for everything, we are out of tune;
It moves us not. — Great God! I 'd rather be
10 A Pagan suckled in a creed outworn;
So might I, standing on this pleasant lea,
Have glimpses that would make me less forlorn;
Have sight of Proteus rising from the sea,
Or hear old Triton blow his wreathèd horn.

YARROW UNVISITED.

See the various Poems the scene of which is laid upon the banks of the Yarrow; in particular, the exquisite Ballad of Hamilton beginning, —

> "Busk ye, busk ye, my bonny, bonny Bride,
> Busk ye, busk ye, my winsome Marrow!"

FROM Stirling Castle we had seen
The mazy Forth unravelled;
Had trod the banks of Clyde and Tay,
And with the Tweed had travelled;
5 And when we came to Clovenford,
Then said my "*winsome Marrow*,"
"Whate'er betide, we'll turn aside,
And see the braes of Yarrow."

"Let Yarrow folk, frae Selkirk town,
10 Who have been buying, selling,
Go back to Yarrow, 't is their own;
Each maiden to her dwelling!
On Yarrow's banks let herons feed,
Hares couch, and rabbits burrow!
15 But we will downward with the Tweed,
Nor turn aside to Yarrow.

"There 's Galla Water, Leader Haughs,
Both lying right before us;
And Dryborough, where with chiming Tweed
20 The lintwhites sing in chorus;
There 's pleasant Tiviot-dale, a land
Made blithe with plough and harrow:
Why throw away a needful day
To go in search of Yarrow?

9. **Frae.** Scottish for *from.*

²⁵ " What 's Yarrow but a river bare,
That glides the dark hills under ?
There are a thousand such elsewhere,
As worthy of your wonder."
Strange words they seemed of slight and scorn !
³⁰ My true-love sighed for sorrow ;
And looked me in the face, to think
I thus could speak of Yarrow !

" Oh, green," said I, " are Yarrow's holms,
And sweet is Yarrow flowing !
³⁵ Fair hangs the apple frae the rock,
But we will leave it growing.
O'er hilly path, and open Strath,
We 'll wander Scotland thorough ;
But, though so near, we will not turn
⁴⁰ Into the dale of Yarrow.

"Let beeves and homebred kine partake
The sweets of Burn-mill meadow ;
The swan on still St. Mary's Lake
Float double, swan and shadow !
⁴⁵ We will not see them ; will not go
To-day, nor yet to-morrow ;
Enough, if in our hearts we know
There 's such a place as Yarrow.

" Be Yarrow stream unseen, unknown !
⁵⁰ It must, or we shall rue it:
We have a vision of our own ;
Ah ! why should we undo it ?
The treasured dreams of times long past,
We 'll keep them, winsome Marrow !

⁵⁵ For when we 're there, although 't is fair,
'T will be another Yarrow!

" If care with freezing years should come,
And wandering seem but folly, —
Should we be loth to stir from home,
⁶⁰ And yet be melancholy, —
Should life be dull, and spirits low,
'T will soothe us in our sorrow,
That earth has something yet to show,
The bonny holms of Yarrow!"

YARROW VISITED.

SEPTEMBER, 1814.

AND is this — Yarrow? — *This* the stream
Of which my fancy cherished,
So faithfully, a waking dream?
An image that hath perished!
⁵ Oh, that some Minstrel's harp were near,
To utter notes of gladness,
And chase this silence from the air,
That fills my heart with sadness!

Yet why? — a silvery current flows
¹⁰ With uncontrolled meanderings;
Nor have these eyes by greener hills
Been soothed, in all my wanderings.
And, through her depths, Saint **Mary's Lake**
Is visibly delighted;
¹⁵ For not a feature of those hills
Is in the mirror slighted.

A blue sky bends o'er Yarrow vale,
Save where that pearly whiteness
Is round the rising sun diffused,
20 A tender, hazy brightness ;
Mild dawn of promise ! that excludes
All profitless dejection ;
Though not unwilling here to admit
A pensive recollection.

25 Where was it that the famous flower
Of Yarrow Vale lay bleeding ?
His bed perchance was yon smooth mound
On which the herd is feeding :
And haply from this crystal pool,
30 Now peaceful as the morning,
The Water-wraith ascended thrice,
And gave his doleful warning.

Delicious is the lay that sings
The haunts of happy lovers,
35 The path that leads them to the grove,
The leafy grove that covers :
And pity sanctifies the verse
That paints, by strength of sorrow,
The unconquerable strength of love ;
40 Bear witness, rueful Yarrow !

But thou, that didst appear so fair
To fond imagination,
Dost rival in the light of day
Her delicate creation :
45 Meek loveliness is round thee spread,
A softness still and holy ;

The grace of forest charms decayed,
And pastoral melancholy.

That region left, the vale unfolds
50 Rich groves of lofty stature,
With Yarrow winding through the pomp
Of cultivated nature;
And, rising from those lofty groves,
Behold a ruin hoary!
55 The shattered front of Newark's towers
Renowned in Border story.

Fair scenes for childhood's opening bloom,
For sportive youth to stray in;
For manhood to enjoy his strength,
60 And age to wear away in!
Yon cottage seems a bower of bliss,
A covert for protection
Of tender thoughts, that nestle there, —
The brood of chaste affection.

65 How sweet, on this autumnal day,
The wild-wood fruits to gather,
And on my true-love's forehead plant
A crest of blooming heather!
And what if I inwreathed my own!
70 'T were no offence to reason;
The sober hills thus deck their brows
To meet the wintry season.

I see, — but not by sight alone,
Loved Yarrow, have I won thee;
75 A ray of fancy still survives, —
Her sunshine plays upon thee!

Thy ever-youthful waters keep
A course of lively pleasure ;
And gladsome notes my lips can breathe,
80 Accordant to the measure.

The vapors linger round the heights,
They melt, and soon must vanish ;
One hour is theirs, nor more is mine, —
Sad thought, which I would banish,
85 But that I know, where'er I go,
Thy genuine image, Yarrow!
Will dwell with me, — to heighten joy,
And cheer my mind in sorrow.

YARROW REVISITED.

In the autumn of 1831, my daughter and I set off from Rydal
to visit Sir Walter Scott, before his departure for Italy. We
reached Abbotsford on Monday. How sadly changed did I find
him from the man I had seen so healthy, gay, and hopeful a
few years before, when he said at the inn at Paterdale, in my
presence, his daughter Anne also being there, with Mr. Lock-
hart, my own wife and daughter, and Mr. Quillinan, "I mean
to live till I am *eighty*," "and shall write as long as I live."
Though we had none of us the least thought of the cloud of
misfortune which was then going to break upon his head, I was
startled, and almost shocked, at that bold saying, which could
scarcely be uttered by such a man, sanguine as he was, without
a momentary forgetfulness of the instability of human life.

But to return to Abbotsford. On Tuesday morning, Sir Walter Scott accompanied us, and most of the party, to Newark
Castle, on the *Yarrow*. When we alighted from the carriages
he walked pretty stoutly, and had great pleasure in revisiting
these his favorite haunts. Of that excursion, the verses *Yarrow
Revisited* are a memorial.

THE gallant youth, who may have gained,
Or seeks, a " winsome Marrow,"

Was but an infant in the lap
When first I looked on Yarrow;
5 Once more, by Newark's castle-gate
Long left without a warder,
I stood, looked, listened, and with thee,
Great Minstrel of the Border!

Grave thoughts ruled wide on that sweet day,
10   Their dignity installing
In gentle bosoms, while sere leaves
Were on the bough, or falling;
But breezes played, and sunshine gleamed,
The forest to embolden;
15 Reddened the fiery hues, and shot
Transparence through the golden.

For busy thoughts the stream flowed on
In foamy agitation;
And slept in many a crystal pool
20   For quiet contemplation:
No public and no private care
The freeborn mind enthralling,
We made a day of happy hours,
Our happy days recalling.

25 Brisk youth appeared, the morn of youth,
With freaks of graceful folly, —
Life's temperate noon, her sober eve,
Her night not melancholy;
Past, present, future, all appeared
30   In harmony united,
Like guests that meet, and some from far,
By cordial love invited.

And if, as Yarrow, through the woods
    And down the meadow ranging,
35 Did meet us with unaltered face,
    Though we were changed and changing;
If, then, some natural shadows spread
    Our inward prospect over,
The soul's deep valley was not slow
40   Its brightness to recover.

Eternal blessings on the Muse,
    And her divine employment!
The blameless Muse, who trains her sons
    For hope and calm enjoyment;
45 Albeit sickness, lingering yet,
    Has o'er their pillow brooded;
And care waylays their steps, — a Sprite
    Not easily eluded.

For thee, O Scott! compelled to change
50   Green Eildon Hill and Cheviot
For warm Vesuvio's vine-clad slopes;
    And leave thy Tweed and Teviot
For mild Sorrento's breezy waves;
    May classic Fancy, linking
55 With native Fancy her fresh aid,
    Preserve thy heart from sinking!

Oh, while they minister to thee,
    Each vying with the other,
May health return to mellow age,
60   With strength, her venturous brother;
And Tiber, and each brook and rill
    Renowned in song and story,

With unimagined beauty shine,
    Nor lose one ray of glory!

65 For thou, upon a hundred streams,
    By tales of love and sorrow,
Of faithful love, undaunted truth,
    Hast shed the power of Yarrow;
And streams unknown, hills yet unseen,
70   Wherever they invite thee,
At parent Nature's grateful call,
    With gladness must requite thee.

A gracious welcome shall be thine,
    Such looks of love and honor
75 As thy own Yarrow gave to me
    When first I gazed upon her;
Beheld what I had feared to see,
    Unwilling to surrender
Dreams treasured up from early days,
80   The holy and the tender.

And what, for this frail world, were all
    That mortals do or suffer,
Did no responsive harp, no pen,
    Memorial tribute offer?
85 Yea, what were mighty Nature's self?
    Her features, could they win us,
Unhelped by the poetic voice
    That hourly speaks within us?

Nor deem that localized Romance
90   Plays false with our affections;
Unsanctifies our tears, — made sport
    For fanciful dejections:

Ah, no! the visions of the past
Sustain the heart in feeling
95 Life as she is, — our changeful life,
With friends and kindred dealing.

Bear witness, ye, whose thoughts that day
In Yarrow's groves were centred ;
Who through the silent portal arch
100 Of mouldering Newark entered ;
And clomb the winding stair that once
Too timidly was mounted
By the "last Minstrel" (not the last!)
Ere he his tale recounted.

105 Flow on forever, Yarrow Stream!
Fulfil thy pensive duty,
Well pleased that future bards should chant
For simple hearts thy beauty ;
To dream-light dear while yet unseen,
110 Dear to the common sunshine,
And dearer still, as now I feel,
To memory's shadowy moonshine!

ON THE DEPARTURE OF SIR WALTER SCOTT FROM ABBOTSFORD, FOR NAPLES.

A TROUBLE, not of clouds, or weeping rain,
Nor of the setting sun's pathetic light
Engendered, hangs o'er Eildon's triple height :
Spirits of power, assembled there, complain
5 For kindred power departing from their sight ;
While Tweed, best pleased in chanting a blithe strain,

Saddens his voice again, and yet again.
Lift up your hearts, ye mourners! for the might
Of the whole world's good wishes with him goes;
10 Blessings and prayers, in nobler retinue
Than sceptred king or laurelled conqueror knows,
Follow this wondrous potentate. Be true,
Ye winds of ocean, and the midland sea,
Wafting your charge to soft Parthenope!

TO A HIGHLAND GIRL.

(AT INVERSNEYDE, UPON LOCH LOMOND.)

SWEET Highland Girl, a very shower
Of beauty is thy earthly dower!
Twice seven consenting years have shed
Their utmost bounty on thy head:
5 And these gray rocks; that household lawn;
Those trees, a veil just half withdrawn;
This fall of water that doth make
A murmur near the silent lake;
This little bay: a quiet road
10 That holds in shelter thy abode;
In truth together do ye seem
Like something fashioned in a dream;
Such forms as from their covert peep
When earthly cares are laid asleep!
15 But, O fair creature! in the light
Of common day, so heavenly bright,
I bless thee, Vision as thou art,
I bless thee with a human heart;
God shield thee to thy latest years!

20 Thee neither know I, nor thy peers :
And yet my eyes are filled with tea···

With earnest feeling I shall play
For thee when I am far away :
For never saw I mien, or face,
25 In which more plainly I could trace
Benignity and homebred sense
Ripening in perfect innocence.
Here scattered, like a random seed,
Remote from men, thou dost not need
30 The embarrassed look of shy distress,
And maidenly shamefacedness :
Thou wear'st upon thy forehead clear
The freedom of a mountaineer :
A face with gladness overspread !
35 Soft smiles, by human kindness bred !
And seemliness complete, that sways
Thy courtesies, about thee plays ;
With no restraint, but such as springs
From quick and eager visitings
40 Of thoughts that lie beyond the reach
Of thy few words of English speech :
A bondage sweetly brooked, a strife
That gives thy gestures grace and life !
So have I, not unmoved in mind,
45 Seen birds of tempest-loving kind
Thus beating up against the wind.

What hand but would a garland cull
For thee who art so beautiful ?
Oh, happy pleasure ! here to dwell
50 Beside thee in some heathy dell ;

Adopt your homely ways, and dress,
A Shepherd, thou a Shepherdess!
But I could frame a wish for thee
More like a grave reality:
55 Thou art to me but as a wave
Of the wild sea; and I would have
Some claim upon thee, if I could,
Though but of common neighborhood.
What joy to hear thee, and to see!
60 Thy elder brother I would be,
Thy father, — anything to thee!

Now thanks to Heaven, that of its grace
Hath led me to this lonely place.
Joy have I had; and going hence
65 I bear away my recompense.
In spots like these it is we prize
Our memory, feel that she hath eyes:
Then, why should I be loth to stir?
I feel this place was made for her;
70 To give new pleasure like the past,
Continued long as life shall last.
Nor am I loth, though pleased at heart,
Sweet Highland Girl! from thee to part;
For I, methinks, till I grow old,
75 As fair before me shall behold,
As I do now, the cabin small,
The lake, the bay, the waterfall;
And thee, the Spirit of them all!

STEPPING WESTWARD.

While my Fellow-traveller and I were walking by the side of
Loch Ketterine, one fine evening after sunset, in our road to a
hut where, in the course of our tour, we had been hospitably
entertained some weeks before, we met, in one of the loneliest
parts of that solitary region, two well-dressed women, one of
whom said to us, by way of greeting, "What, you are stepping
westward ?"

" *What, you are stepping westward?* " — " *Yea.*"
— 'T would be a *wildish* destiny,
If we, who thus together roam
In a strange land, and far from home,
5 Were in this place the guests of chance :
Yet who would stop, or fear to advance,
Though home or shelter he had none,
With such a sky to lead him on ?

The dewy ground was dark and cold ;
10 Behind, all gloomy to behold ;
And stepping westward seemed to be
A kind of *heavenly* destiny :
I liked the greeting ; 't was a sound
Of something without place or bound ;
15 And seemed to give me spiritual right
To travel through that region bright.

The voice was soft, and she who spake
Was walking by her native lake :
The salutation had to me
20 The very sound of courtesy :
Its power was felt ; and while my eye
Was fixed upon the glowing sky,

The echo of the voice inwrought
A human sweetness with the thought
25 Of travelling through the world that lay
Before me in my endless way.

THE SOLITARY REAPER.

BEHOLD her, single in the field,
You solitary Highland Lass!
Reaping and singing by herself;
Stop here, or gently pass!
5 Alone she cuts and binds the grain,
And sings a melancholy strain;
Oh, listen! for the vale profound
Is overflowing with the sound.

No nightingale did ever chant
10 More welcome notes to weary bands
Of travellers in some shady haunt,
Among Arabian sands:
A voice so thrilling ne'er was heard
In spring-time from the cuckoo-bird,
15 Breaking the silence of the seas
Among the farthest Hebrides.

Will no one tell me what she sings? —
Perhaps the plaintive numbers flow
For old, unhappy, far-off things,
20 And battles long ago:
Or is it some more humble lay,
Familiar matter of to-day?
Some natural sorrow, loss, or pain,
That has been, and may be again?

25 Whate'er the theme, the maiden sang
As if her song could have no ending;
I saw her singing at her work,
And o'er the sickle bending; —
I listened, motionless and still;
30 And, as I mounted up the hill,
The music in my heart I bore,
Long after it was heard no more.

SONNET,

COMPOSED UPON WESTMINSTER BRIDGE.

EARTH has not anything to show more fair:
Dull would he be of soul who could pass by
A sight so touching in its majesty:
This City now doth, like a garment, wear
5 The beauty of the morning; silent, bare,
Ships, towers, domes, theatres, and temples lie
Open unto the fields, and to the sky,
All bright and glittering in the smokeless air.
Never did sun more beautifully steep,
10 In his first splendor, valley, rock, or hill;
Ne'er saw I, never felt, a calm so deep!
The river glideth at his own sweet will:
Dear God! the very houses seem asleep;
And all that mighty heart is lying still!

TO SLEEP.

A FLOCK of sheep that leisurely pass by,
One after one; the sound of rain, and bees
Murmuring; the fall of rivers, winds and seas,

Smooth fields, white sheets of water, and pure sky;
5 I have thought of all by turns, and yet to lie
Sleepless! and soon the small birds' melodies
Must hear, first uttered from my orchard trees;
And the first cuckoo's melancholy cry.
Even thus last night, and two nights more, I lay,
10 And could not win thee, Sleep! by any stealth;
So do not let me wear to-night away:
Without thee what is all the morning's wealth?
Come, blessed barrier between day and day,
Dear mother of fresh thoughts and joyous health!

IT IS A BEAUTEOUS EVENING, CALM AND FREE.

It is a beauteous evening, calm and free,
The holy time is quiet as a nun
Breathless with adoration; the broad sun
Is sinking down in its tranquillity;
5 The gentleness of heaven broods o'er the sea.
Listen! the mighty Being is awake,
And doth with his eternal motion make
A sound like thunder — everlastingly.
Dear child! dear girl! that walkest with me here,
10 If thou appear untouched by solemn thought,
Thy nature is not therefore less divine:
Thou liest in Abraham's bosom all the year;
And worshipp'st at the temple's inner shrine,
God being with thee when we know it not.

ELEGIAC STANZAS,

SUGGESTED BY A PICTURE OF PEELE CASTLE IN A STORM,
PAINTED BY SIR GEORGE BEAUMONT.

I was thy neighbor once, thou rugged Pile!
Four summer weeks I dwelt in sight of thee :
I saw thee every day; and all the while
Thy form was sleeping on a glassy sea.

5 So pure the sky, so quiet was the air!
So like, so very like, was day to day!
Whene'er I looked, thy image still was there;
It trembled, but it never passed away.

How perfect was the calm! it seemed no sleep;
10 No mood, which season takes away, or brings :
I could have fancied that the mighty Deep
Was even the gentlest of all gentle things.

Ah! then, if mine had been the Painter's hand,
To express what then I saw; and add the gleam,
15 The light that never was, on sea or land,
The consecration, and the Poet's dream ;

I would have planted thee, thou hoary Pile,
Amid a world how different from this!
Beside a sea that could not cease to smile ;
20 On tranquil land, beneath a sky of bliss.

Thou shouldst have seemed a treasure-house divine
Of peaceful years; a chronicle of heaven ; —
Of all the sunbeams that did ever shine,
The very sweetest had to thee been given.

25 A picture had it been of lasting ease,
  Elysian quiet, without toil or strife;
  No motion but the moving tide, a breeze,
  Or merely silent Nature's breathing life.

  Such, in the fond illusion of my heart,
30 Such picture would I at that time have made:
  And seen the soul of truth in every part,
  A steadfast peace that might not be betrayed.

  So once it would have been, — 't is so no more;
  I have submitted to a new control;
35 A power is gone, which nothing can restore;
  A deep distress hath humanized my soul.

  Not for a moment could I now behold
  A smiling sea, and be what I have been:
  The feeling of my loss will ne'er be old;
40 This, which I know, I speak with mind serene.

  Then, Beaumont, friend! who would have been
      the friend,
  If he had lived, of him whom I deplore,
  This work of thine I blame not, but commend;
  This sea in anger, and that dismal shore.

45 Oh, 't is a passionate work! — yet wise and well,
  Well chosen is the spirit that is here;
  That hulk which labors in the deadly swell,
  This rueful sky, this pageantry of fear!

42. Wordsworth's brother John, who had lately been lost at
sea.

And this huge castle, standing here sublime,
50 I love to see the look with which it braves,
Cased in the unfeeling armor of old time,
The lightning, the fierce wind, and trampling
waves.

Farewell, farewell the heart that lives alone,
Housed in a dream, at distance from the kind!
55 Such happiness, wherever it be known,
Is to be pitied; for 't is surely blind.

But welcome fortitude, and patient cheer,
And frequent sights of what is to be borne!
Such sights, or worse, as are before me here. —
60 Not without hope we suffer and we mourn.

A POET'S EPITAPH.

ART thou a Statist, in the van
Of public conflicts trained and bred?
First learn to love one living man;
Then mayst thou think upon the dead.

5 A Lawyer art thou? — draw not nigh!
Go, carry to some fitter place
The keenness of that practised eye,
The hardness of that sallow face.

Art thou a Man of purple cheer?
10 A rosy Man, right plump to see?
Approach! yet. Doctor, not too near:
This grave no cushion is for thee.

Or art thou one of gallant pride,
A Soldier and no man of chaff ?
15 Welcome ! — but lay thy sword aside,
And lean upon a peasant's staff.

Physician art thou ? — one all eyes,
Philosopher ! — a fingering slave,
One that would peep and botanize
20 Upon his mother's grave ?

Wrapt closely in thy sensual fleece,
O!., turn aside, — and take, I pray,
That he below may rest in peace,
Thy ever-dwindling soul away !

25 A Moralist perchance appears ;
Led, Heaven knows how ! to this poor sod ;
And he has neither eyes nor ears ;
Himself his world, and his own God ;

One to whose smooth-rubbed soul can cling
30 Nor form, nor feeling, great or small ;
A reasoning, self-sufficing thing,
An intellectual All-in-all !

Shut close the door ; press down the latch ;
Sleep in thy intellectual crust :
35 Nor lose ten tickings of thy watch
Near this unprofitable dust.

But who is he, with modest looks,
And clad in homely russet-brown ?
He murmurs near the running brooks
40 A music sweeter than their own.

He is retired as noontide dew,
Or fountain in a noonday grove;
And you must love him, ere to you
He will seem worthy of your love.

45 The outward shows of sky and earth,
Of hill and valley, he has viewed;
And impulses of deeper birth
Have come to him in solitude.

In common things that round us lie
50 Some random truths he can impart,
The harvest of a quiet eye,
That broods and sleeps on his own heart.

But he is weak; both Man and Boy,
Hath been an idler in the land,
55 Contented if he might enjoy
The things which others understand.

— Come hither in thy hour of strength;
Come, weak as is a breaking wave!
Here stretch thy body at full length;
60 Or build thy house upon this grave.

EXTEMPORE EFFUSION UPON THE DEATH OF JAMES HOGG.

WHEN first, descending from the moorlands,
I saw the stream of Yarrow glide
Along a bare and open valley,
The Ettrick Shepherd was my guide.

4. James Hogg was a shepherd in the Vale of Ettrick, who had a slight but genuine poetic gift. He was a friend of Walter Scott's.

5 When last along its banks I wandered,
 Through groves that had begun to shed
 Their golden leaves upon the pathways,
 My steps the Border-minstrel led.

 The mighty Minstrel breathes no longer,
10 'Mid mouldering ruins low he lies;
 And death upon the braes of Yarrow
 Has closed the Shepherd-poet's eyes;

 Nor has the rolling year twice measured,
 From sign to sign, its steadfast course,
15 Since every mortal power of Coleridge
 Was frozen at its marvellous source;

 The rapt one, of the godlike forehead,
 The heaven-eyed creature sleeps in earth;
 And Lamb, the frolic and the gentle,
20 Has vanished from his lonely hearth.

 Like clouds that rake the mountain-summits,
 Or waves that own no curbing hand,
 How fast has brother followed brother,
 From sunshine to the sunless land!

25 Yet I, whose lids from infant slumber
 Were earlier raised, remain to hear
 A timid voice, that asks in whispers,
 "Who next will drop and disappear?"

 Our haughty life is crowned with darkness,
30 Like London with its own black wreath,
 On which, with thee, O Crabbe! forth-looking,
 I gazed from Hampstead's breezy heath.

As if but yesterday departed,
Thou too art gone before ; but why,
35 O'er ripe fruit, seasonably gathered,
Should frail survivors heave a sigh?

Mourn rather for that holy Spirit,
Sweet as the spring, as ocean deep ;
For her who, ere her summer faded,
40 Has sunk into a breathless sleep.

No more of old romantic sorrows,
For slaughtered youth or love-lorn maid !
With sharper grief is Yarrow smitten,
And Ettrick mourns with her their Poet dead.

RESOLUTION AND INDEPENDENCE.

THERE was a roaring in the wind all night ;
The rain came heavily and fell in floods ;
But now the sun is rising calm and bright ;
The birds are singing in the distant woods ;
5 Over his own sweet voice the stock-dove broods ;
The jay makes answer as the magpie chatters ;
And all the air is filled with pleasant noise of waters.

All things that love the sun are out of doors ;
The sky rejoices in the morning's birth ;
10 The grass is bright with rain-drops ; — on the moors
The hare is running races in her mirth ;
And with her feet she from the plashy earth
Raises a mist ; that, glittering in the sun,
Runs with her all the way, wherever she doth run.

39. Felicia Hemans.

15 I was a Traveller then upon the moor;
  I saw the hare that raced about with joy;
  I heard the woods and distant waters roar;
  Or heard them not, as happy as a boy:
  The pleasant season did my heart employ:
20 My old remembrances went from me wholly;
  And all the ways of men, so vain and melancholy.

But, as it sometimes chanceth, from the might
  Of joy in minds that can no further go,
  As high as we have mounted in delight
25 In our dejection do we sink as low;
  To me that morning did it happen so;
  And fears and fancies thick upon me came;
  Dim sadness, and blind thoughts, I knew not, nor
      could name.

I heard the skylark warbling in the sky;
30 And I bethought me of the playful hare:
  Even such a happy child of earth am I;
  Even as these blissful creatures do I fare;
  Far from the world I walk, and all from care;
  But there may come another day to me,—
35 Solitude, pain of heart, distress, and poverty.

My whole life I have lived in pleasant thought,
  As if life's business were a summer mood;
  As if all needful things would come unsought
  To genial faith, still rich in genial good;
40 But how can he expect that others should
  Build for him, sow for him, and at his call
  Love him, who for himself will take no heed at
      all?

I thought of Chatterton, the marvellous Boy,
The sleepless soul that perished in his pride ;
45 Of him who walked in glory and in joy,
Following his plough, along the mountain-side :
By our own spirits we are deified :
We Poets in our youth begin in gladness ;
But thereof come in the end despondency and mad-
ness.

50 Now, whether it were by peculiar grace,
A leading from above, a something given,
Yet it befell, that, in this lonely place,
When I with these untoward thoughts had striven,
Beside a pool bare to the eye of heaven,
55 I saw a man before me unawares :
The oldest man he seemed that ever wore gray hairs.

As a huge stone is sometimes seen to lie
Couched on the bald top of an eminence,
Wonder to all who do the same espy,
60 By what means it could thither come, and whence :
So that it seems a thing endued with sense ; —
Like a sea-beast crawled forth, that on a shelf
Of rock or sand reposeth, there to sun itself ; —

Such seemed this man, not all alive nor dead,
65 Nor all asleep, in his extreme old age :
His body was bent double, feet and head
Coming together in life's pilgrimage ;
As if some dire constraint of pain, or rage
Of sickness felt by him in times long past,
70 A more than human weight upon his frame had
cast.

45. Robert Burns.

Himself he propped, limbs, body, and pale face,
Upon a long gray staff of shaven wood :
And, still as I drew near with gentle pace,
Upon the margin of that moorish flood
75 Motionless as a cloud the old man stood,
That heareth not the loud winds when they call,
And moveth all together, if it move at all.

At length, himself unsettling, he the pond
Stirred with his staff, and fixedly did look
80 Upon that muddy water, which he conned,
As if he had been reading in a book :
And now a stranger's privilege I took ;
And, drawing to his side, to him did say,
" This morning gives us promise of a glorious day."

85 A gentle answer did the old man make,
In courteous speech which forth he slowly drew ;
And him with further words I thus bespake :
" What occupation do you there pursue ?
This is a lonesome place for one like you."
90 Ere he replied, a flash of mild surprise
Broke from the sable orbs of his yet vivid eyes.

His words came feebly, from a feeble chest,
But each in solemn order followed each,
With something of a lofty utterance drest, —
95 Choice word and measured phrase, above the reach
Of ordinary men ; a stately speech ;
Such as grave livers do in Scotland use,
Religious men, who give to God and man their dues.

He told, that to these waters he had come
100 To gather leeches, being old and poor :

Employment hazardous and wearisome !
And he had many hardships to endure :
From pond to pond he roamed, from moor to moor ;
Housing, with God's good help, by choice or chance;
105 And in this way he gained an honest maintenance.

The old man still stood talking by my side ;
But now his voice to me was like a stream
Scarce heard ; nor word from word could I divide ;
And the whole body of the man did seem
110 Like one whom I had met with in a dream ;
Or like a man from some far region sent,
To give me human strength, by apt admonishment.

My former thoughts returned: the fear that kills
And hope that is unwilling to be fed ;
115 Cold, pain, and labor, and all fleshly ills ;
And mighty poets in their misery dead.
— Perplexed, and longing to be comforted,
My question eagerly did I renew,
" How is it that you live, and what is it you do ? "

120 He with a smile did then his words repeat ;
And said, that, gathering leeches, far and wide
He travelled ; stirring thus about his feet
The waters of the pools where they abide.
" Once I could meet with them on every side ;
125 But they have dwindled long by slow decay ;
Yet still I persevere, and find them where I may."

While he was talking thus, the lonely place,
The old man's shape, and speech, — all troubled
     me :
In my mind's eye I seemed to see him pace

130 About the weary moors continually,
Wandering about alone and silently.
While I these thoughts within myself pursued,
He, having made a pause, the same discourse re-
newed.

And soon with this he other matter blended,
135 Cheerfully uttered, with demeanor kind,
But stately in the main ; and when he ended,
I could have laughed myself to scorn, to find
In that decrepit man so firm a mind.
" God," said I, " be my help and stay secure ;
140 I 'll think of the Leech-gatherer on the lonely moor ! "

ODE TO DUTY.

STERN Daughter of the Voice of God !
O Duty ! if that name thou love,
Who art a light to guide, a rod
To check the erring, and reprove
5 Thou, who art victory and law
When empty terrors overawe,
From vain temptations dost set free,
And calm'st the weary strife of frail humanity !

There are who ask not if thine eye
10 Be on them ; who, in love and truth,
Where no misgiving is, rely
Upon the genial sense of youth :
Glad hearts ! without reproach or blot ;
Who do thy work, and know it not :
15 Oh ! if through confidence misplaced
They fail, thy saving arms, dread Power ! around
them cast.

Serene will be our days and bright,
And happy will our nature be,
When love is an unerring light,
20 And joy its own security.
And they a blissful course may hold
Even now, who, not unwisely bold,
Live in the spirit of this creed ;
Yet seek thy firm support, according to their need.

25 I, loving freedom, and untried,
No sport of every random gust,
Yet being to myself a guide,
Too blindly have reposed my trust :
And oft, when in my heart was heard
30 Thy timely mandate, I deferred
The task, in smoother walks to stray ;
But thee I now would serve more strictly, if I
  may.

Through no disturbance of my soul,
Or strong compunction in me wrought,
35 I supplicate for thy control ;
But in the quietness of thought :
Me this unchartered freedom tires ;
I feel the weight of chance-desires :
My hopes no more must change their name,
40 I long for a repose that ever is the same.

Stern Lawgiver ! yet thou dost wear
The Godhead's most benignant grace ;
Nor know we anything so fair
As is the smile upon thy face :
45 Flowers laugh before thee on their beds,
And fragrance in thy footing treads ;

Thou dost preserve the stars from wrong;
And the most ancient heavens, through Thee, are
  fresh and strong.

To humbler functions, awful Power!
50 I call thee: I myself commend
Unto thy guidance from this hour;
Oh, let my weakness have an end!
Give unto me, made lowly wise,
The spirit of self-sacrifice:
55 The confidence of reason give;
And in the light of truth thy Bondman let me
  live.

CHARACTER OF THE HAPPY WARRIOR.

Many elements of the character here portrayed were found in
my brother John, who perished by shipwreck. His messmates
used to call him *the Philosopher*, from which it may be inferred
that the qualities and dispositions I allude to had not escaped
their notice. He greatly valued moral and religious instruction
for youth, as tending to make good sailors. The best, he used
to say, came from Scotland; the next to them, from the North
of England, especially from Westmoreland and Cumberland,
where, thanks to the piety and local attachments of our ances-
tors, endowed, or, as they are called, free schools, abound.

Who is the happy Warrior? Who is he
That every man in arms should wish to be?
— It is the generous spirit, who, when brought
Among the tasks of real life, hath wrought
5 Upon the plan that pleased his boyish thought:
Whose high endeavors are an inward light
That makes the path before him always bright:
Who, with a natural instinct to discern

What knowledge can perform, is diligent to learn;
10 Abides by this resolve, and stops not there,
But makes his moral being his prime care ;
Who, doomed to go in company with pain,
And fear, and bloodshed, miserable train !
Turns his necessity to glorious gain ;
15 In face of these doth exercise a power
Which is our human nature's highest dower ;
Controls them and subdues, transmutes, bereaves
Of their bad influence, and their good receives :
By objects, which might force the soul to abate
20 Her feeling, rendered more compassionate ;
Is placable, — because occasions rise
So often that demand such sacrifice ;
More skilful in self-knowledge, even more pure,
As tempted more ; more able to endure,
25 As more exposed to suffering and distress ;
Thence, also, more alive to tenderness :
— 'T is he whose law is reason ; who depends
Upon that law as on the best of friends ;
Whence, in a state where men are tempted still
30 To evil for a guard against worse ill,
And what in quality or act is best
Doth seldom on a right foundation rest ;
He labors good on good to fix, and owes
To virtue every triumph that he knows :
35 — Who, if he rise to station of command,
Rises by open means ; and there will stand
On honorable terms, or else retire,
And in himself possess his own desire :
Who comprehends his trust, and to the same
40 Keeps faithful with a singleness of aim ;
And therefore does not stoop, nor lie in wait
For wealth, or honors, or for worldly state ;

Whom they must follow, on whose head must fall,
Like showers of manna, if they come at all:
45 Whose powers shed round him in the common strife,
Or mild concerns of ordinary life,
A constant influence, a peculiar grace;
But who, if he be called upon to face
Some awful moment to which Heaven has joined
50 Great issues, good or bad for human kind,
Is happy as a lover; and attired
With sudden brightness, like a man inspired;
And, through the heat of conflict, keeps the law
In calmness made, and sees what he foresaw;
55 Or if an unexpected call succeed,
Come when it will, is equal to the need:
— He who, though thus endued as with a sense
And faculty for storm and turbulence,
Is yet a Soul whose master-bias leans
60 To homefelt pleasures and to gentle scenes;
Sweet images! which, wheresoe'er he be,
Are at his heart; and such fidelity
It is his darling passion to approve;
More brave for this, that he hath much to love: —
65 'T is, finally, the man, who, lifted high,
Conspicuous object in a nation's eye,
Or left unthought of in obscurity, —
Who, with a toward or untoward lot,
Prosperous or adverse, to his wish or not,
70 Plays, in the many games of life, that one
Where what he most doth value must be won:
Whom neither shape of danger can dismay,
Nor thought of tender happiness betray;
Who, not content that former worth stand fast,
75 Looks forward, persevering to the last,
From well to better, daily self-surpast:

Who, whether praise of him must walk the earth
Forever, and to noble deeds give birth,
Or he must fall, to sleep without his fame,
80 And leave a dead, unprofitable name,
Finds comfort in himself and in his cause ;
And, while the mortal mist is gathering, draws
His breath in confidence of Heaven's applause, —
This is the happy Warrior ; this is he
85 That every man in arms should wish to be.

MY HEART LEAPS UP.

My heart leaps up when I behold
   A rainbow in the sky :
So was it when my life began ;
So is it now I am a man ;
So be it when I shall grow old,
   Or let me die !
The child is father of the man ;
And I could wish my days to be
Bound each to each by natural piety.

ODE :

INTIMATIONS OF IMMORTALITY FROM RECOL-
LECTIONS OF EARLY CHILDHOOD.

INTRODUCTORY NOTE.

WORDSWORTH used the closing lines of the poem
last given as a motto to his great Ode, and in his pref-
ace he says : " To the attentive and competent reader,
the whole sufficiently explains itself, but there may
be no harm in adverting here to particular feelings or
experiences of my own mind, on which the structure
of the poem partly rests. Nothing was more difficult
for me in childhood than to admit the notion of death
as a state applicable to my own being. I have said
elsewhere

'A simple Child,
That lightly draws its breath,
And feels its life in every limb,
What should it know of death ? '

But it was not so much from the source of animal
vivacity that *my* difficulty came, as from a sense of
the indomitableness of the spirit within me. I used
to brood over the stories of Enoch and Elijah, and
almost persuade myself that, whatever might become
of others, I should be translated in something of the
same way to heaven. With a feeling congenial to
this, I was often unable to think of external things as
having external existence, and I communed with all
that I saw as something not apart from, but inherent
in, my own immaterial nature. Many times while

going to school have I grasped at a wall or tree to recall myself from this abyss of idealism to the reality. At that time I was afraid of such processes. In later periods of life I have deplored, as we have all reason to do, a subjugation of an opposite character. . . . To that dream-like vividness and splendor which invest objects of sight in childhood, every one, I believe, if he would look back, could bear testimony, and I need not dwell upon it here; but having in the poem regarded it as presumptive evidence of a prior state of existence, I think it right to protest against a conclusion, which has given pain to some good and pious persons, that I meant to inculcate such a belief. · It is far too shadowy a notion to be recommended to faith as more than an element in our instincts of immortality. But let us bear in mind that, though the idea is not advanced in revelation, there is nothing there to contradict it, and the fall of man presents an analogy in its favor. Accordingly, a preëxistent state has entered into the popular creeds of many nations, and among all persons acquainted with classic literature is known as an ingredient in Platonic philosophy. Archimedes said that he could move the world if he had a point whereon to rest his machine. Who has not felt the same aspirations as regards the world of his own mind? Having to wield some of its elements when I was impelled to write this poem on the ' Immortality of the Soul,' I took hold of the notion of preëxistence as having sufficient foundation in humanity for authorizing me to make for my purpose the best use of it I could as a Poet."

Possibly Wordsworth has laid too much stress on the part which this theory of preëxistence plays in the Ode. His artistic presentation is better than his philosophizing. The confusion into which some have been cast by the Ode arises from their bringing to the idea of immortality the time conception; they conceive the poet to be hinting of an indefinite time antedating the child's birth, an indefinite time extending beyond the man's death, whereas Wordsworth's conception of immortality rests in the indestructibility of spirit by any temporal or earthly conditions, — an indestructibility which even implies an absence of beginning as well as of ending.

" Heaven lies about us in our infancy,"

he declares. It is the investment of this visible life by an unseen, unfelt, yet real spiritual presence for which he contends, and he maintains that the inmost consciousness of childhood bears witness to this truth; this consciousness fades as the earthly life penetrates the soul, yet it is there, and recurs in sudden moments.

In printing the Ode, Wordsworth's capitalizing, which was partly a fashion of the day and partly characteristic of his own habit of mind, has been followed.

ODE.

I.

THERE was a time when meadow, grove, and stream,
The earth, and every common sight,
    To me did seem
    Apparelled in celestial light,
5 The glory and the freshness of a dream.
It is not now as it hath been of yore ; —
    Turn wheresoe'er I may,
    By night or day,
The things which I have seen I now can see no more.

II.

10   The Rainbow comes and goes,
    And lovely is the Rose ;
    The Moon doth with delight
Look round her when the heavens are bare ;
    Waters on a starry night
15   Are beautiful and fair;
    The sunshine is a glorious birth ;
    But yet I know where'er I go,
That there hath passed away a glory from the earth.

III.

v, while the birds thus sing a joyous song,
    And while the young lambs bound
    As to the tabor's sound,
me alone there came a thought of grief :

A timely utterance gave that thought relief,
    And I again am strong:
25 The cataracts blow their trumpets from the steep;
No more shall grief of mine the season wrong;
I hear the echoes through the mountains throng,
The winds come to me from the fields of sleep,
    And all the earth is gay;
30   Land and sea
    Give themselves up to jollity,
    And with the heart of May
    Doth every beast keep holiday; —
      Thou Child of Joy.
35 Shout round me, let me hear thy shouts, thou happy
    Shepherd-boy!

IV.

Ye blessed Creatures, I have heard the call
    Ye to each other make; I see
The heavens laugh with you in your jubilee;
    My heart is at your festival,
40   My head hath its coronal,
The fulness of your bliss, I feel, I feel it all.
    O evil day! if I were sullen
    While Earth herself is adorning,
      This sweet May morning,
45   And the Children are culling
      On every side,
    In a thousand valleys far and wide,
    Fresh flowers; while the sun shines warm,
And the Babe leaps up on his Mother's arm: —
50   I hear, I hear, with joy I hear!
    — But there's a Tree, of many, one,
A single Field which I have looked upon,
Both of them speak of something that is gone:

The pansy at my feet
55   Doth the same tale repeat :
Whither is fled the visionary gleam ?
Where is it now, the glory and the dream ?

V.

Our birth is but a sleep and a forgetting :
The Soul that rises with us, our life's Star,
60   Hath had elsewhere its setting,
      And cometh from afar :
      Not in entire forgetfulness,
      And not in utter nakedness,
But trailing clouds of glory, do we come
65   From God, who is our home :
Heaven lies about us in our infancy !
Shades of the prison-house begin to close
      Upon the growing Boy,
But he beholds the light, and whence it flows,
70   He sees it in his joy ;
The Youth, who daily farther from the east
      Must travel, still is Nature's Priest,
      And by the vision splendid
      Is on his way attended ;
75 At length the Man perceives it die away,
And fade into the light of common day.

VI.

Earth fills her lap with pleasures of her own ;
Yearnings she hath in her own natural kind,
And, even with something of a Mother's mind,
80   And no unworthy aim,
      The homely Nurse doth all she can
To make her Foster-child, her Inmate Man,
      Forget the glories he hath known,
And that imperial palace whence he came.

VII.

85 Behold the Child among his new-born blisses,
A six years' Darling of a pigmy size!
See, where 'mid work of his own hand he lies,
Fretted by sallies of his mother's kisses,
With light upon him from his father's eyes !
90 See, at his feet, some little plan or chart,
Some fragment from his dream of human life,
Shaped by himself with newly-learned art ;
  A wedding or a festival,
  A mourning or a funeral ;
95   And this hath now his heart,
  And unto this he frames his song :
   Then will he fit his tongue
To dialogues of business, love, or strife ;
  But it will not be long
100   Ere this be thrown aside,
  And with new joy and pride
The little Actor cons another part ;
Filling from time to time his " humorous stage "
With all the Persons, down to palsied Age,
105 That Life brings with her in her equipage ;
  As if his whole vocation
  Were endless imitation.

VIII.

Thou, whose exterior semblance doth belie
  Thy Soul's immensity ;
110 Thou best Philosopher, who yet dost keep
Thy heritage, thou Eye among the blind,
That, deaf and silent, read'st the eternal deep,
Haunted forever by the eternal mind, —
  Mighty Prophet ! Seer blest !
115   On whom those truths do rest,

Which we are toiling all our lives to find,
In darkness lost, the darkness of the grave;
Thou, over whom thy Immortality
Broods like the Day, a Master o'er a Slave,
120 A Presence which is not to be put by;
Thou little Child, yet glorious in the might
Of heaven-born freedom on thy being's height,
Why with such earnest pains dost thou provoke
The years to bring the inevitable yoke,
125 Thus blindly with thy blessedness at strife?
Full soon thy Soul shall have her earthly freight,
And custom lie upon thee with a weight,
Heavy as frost, and deep almost as life!

IX.

O joy! that in our embers
130 Is something that doth live,
That Nature yet remembers
What was so fugitive!
The thought of our past years in me doth breed
Perpetual benediction: not indeed
135 For that which is most worthy to be blest;
Delight and liberty, the simple creed
Of Childhood, whether busy or at rest,
With new-fledged hope still fluttering in his breast:
Not for these I raise
140 The song of thanks and praise;
But for those obstinate questionings
Of sense and outward things,
Fallings from us, vanishings;
Blank misgivings of a Creature
145 Moving about in worlds not realized,
High instincts before which our mortal Nature
Did tremble like a guilty thing surprised:

But for those first affections,
Those shadowy recollections,
150   Which, be they what they may,
Are yet the fountain light of all our day,
Are yet a master light of all our seeing ,
Uphold us, cherish, and have power to make
Our noisy years seem moments in the being
155 Of the eternal Silence : truths that wake,
To perish never ;
Which neither listlessness, nor mad endeavor,
Nor Man nor Boy,
Nor all that is at enmity with joy,
160 Can utterly abolish or destroy !
Hence in a season of calm weather,
Though inland far we be,
Our souls have sight of that immortal sea
Which brought us hither,
165   Can in a moment travel thither,
And see the Children sport upon the shore,
And hear the mighty waters rolling evermore.

X.

Then sing, ye Birds, sing, sing a joyous song !
And let the young Lambs bound
170   As to the tabor's sound !
We in thought will join your throng,
Ye that pipe and ye that play,
Ye that through your hearts to-day
Feel the gladness of the May !
175 What   though   the   radiance   which   was   once   so
bright
Be now forever taken from my sight,
Though nothing can bring back the hour
Of splendor in the grass, of glory in the flower;

We will grieve not, rather find
180   Strength in what remains behind;
In the primal sympathy
Which, having been, must ever be;
In the soothing thoughts that spring
Out of human suffering;
135   In the faith that looks through death,
In years that bring the philosophic mind.

XI.

And O ye Fountains, Meadows, Hills, and Groves,
Forebode not any severing of our loves!
Yet in my heart of hearts I feel your might;
190 I only have relinquished one delight
To live beneath your more habitual sway.
I love the Brooks which down their channels fret,
Even more than when I tripped lightly as they;
The innocent brightness of a new-born Day
195   Is lovely yet;
The Clouds that gather round the setting sun
Do take a sober coloring from an eye
That hath kept watch o'er man's mortality;
Another race hath been, and other palms are won.
200 Thanks to the human heart by which we live,
. Thanks to its tenderness, its joys, and fears,
To me the meanest flower that blows can give
Thoughts that do often lie too deep for tears.

LB S '20

The Riverside Literature Series.

[*A list of the first fifty-three numbers is given on the next page.*]

EXTRA NUMBERS.

The Riverside Literature Series.

With Introductions, Notes, Historical Sketches, and Biographical Sketches
Each regular single number, paper, 15 cents.

* 29 and 10 also in one volume, linen, 40 cents: likewise 28 and 36, 4 and 5, 15 and 30, 40 and 69, and 11 and 63. ** Also bound in linen, 25 cents. † Also in one volume linen, 45 cents. ‡ Also in one volume, linen, 40 cents. ‡‡ 1, 4, and 30 also in one volume, linen, 50 cents.

Continued on the inside of this cover.

www.ingramcontent.com/pod-product-compliance
Lightning Source LLC
Chambersburg PA
CBHW020038030726
47499CB00007B/2483